10-5
ALASKA SKIP

10-5
ALASKA SKIP

By Bob Cunningham

Illustrations by: Rod and Barbara Furan

Library of Congress Catalog Card Number: 76-051138. International Standard Book Number: 0-913940-58-5.

TO THE READER: ALL CB TERMS ARE EXPLAINED IN THE GLOSSARY ON PAGES 30-31.

4

Sunlight poured down on Mount Olympus.

"What a view!" said young Ryan Hawkins. He was the first of the climbing party to reach the summit. There he shrugged off his pack and put down his ice axe.

Ryan's sister, Kristi, joined him at the top. Then came their parents, Neil and Sara. The family stood on the windswept ridge and admired the fantastic scene around them.

Dazzling white rivers of ice reached down the flanks of Olympus and its neighbor, Mount Tom. Below that were dark green forests. To the west lay the blue Pacific Ocean. To the east were the islands of Washington's Puget Sound and on the horizon, Mount Rainier.

Ryan exclaimed: "On a day like this, I'll bet you can see all the way to Alaska!"

Neil laughed. "Alaska's panhandle is at least 700 miles away, son. That land to the north is Vancouver Island."

The children took turns using binoculars while Sara began to photograph the beautiful view. Neil opened his pack and took out a CB walkie-talkie.

"Let's tell the Matuccis that we made it to the top." He pressed the mike button. "Break Channel Ten. How about that Italian Stallion? You got your ears on, Carl? Come on back to Sky Hawk, KCW-0484."

Neil released the mike button and listened. He heard a babble of faint voices that all seemed to be talking at once. Mixed in with them were hisses, buzzes, and faint whistles.

"One more time for that Italian Stallion. Pick it up. You got a copy on this Sky Hawk sitting on top of Mount Olympus, come on?"

Once more he waited, but all he heard was the static and the spooky, faraway voices.

"Bodacious skip today," Neil remarked. "The sunspots must be doing their thing." He keyed the mike and tried again. "Anybody got a copy on this one Sky Hawk up on the mountain, come back?"

A voice cut clearly through the hash. "Yo, we got ya, Sky Hawk."

"Who we got here, okay?"

"You got the ole Road Toad outa Port Angeles, good buddy. You're barely making the trip in skipland today. What are you pushing?"

"We got a W-T up here on Mount Olympus. Just made it to the top. You want to try a 10-5 for us, Road Toad? We promised to give some friends a holler once we got up here. They're hanging out on Channel Ten waiting for our shout. Just raise that old Italian Stallion and let him know that Sky Hawk and the gang will be boogying on down now. Okay."

"Glad to do your 10-5, Sky Hawk. You got stomped on there a little. Would you 10-9 on that rascal's handle again, get back?"
"Italian Stallion, KFK-4236."

"Roger-Four fer shore. We'll sort the rascal out with this here hamburger helper of ours. Mercy sakes, we can blow the windows out of any modulator in this end of Washington state if we really put our boots on. You can depend on the one Road Toad!"

"Ten-Four. Thanks very much and 73's to you. This is Sky Hawk, KCW-0484, backin' on out, and we're clear."

"All them good numbers to you, Hawk. Ten-ten till we do it again. We up, we down, we clear, we gone!"

Sara Hawkins had finished taking her photos. She put her camera back into her backpack and remarked: "He certainly did have a loud signal."

Neil gave a wry smile. "Do you know what a hamburger helper is?"

Sara frowned. "I suppose it's one of those thingummies that boost the signal illegally."

"Right. A linear amplifier. CB transmitters are supposed to have no more than four watts for AM sets or twelve watts for sidebanders. Linears can boost the power to hundreds of watts."

"I don't see why they have to be illegal," Ryan said.

"After all," Kristi added, "sometimes you need more than four watts. Sometimes you need to cut through the garbage and get your message through."

Ryan said: "Road Toad and his footwarmer got through to us despite the skip. Could be that Italian Stallion heard us, too. We couldn't hear him because his signal was too weak!"

The Hawkins found a sheltered nook and sat down to eat lunch. The hot soup, sardines, biscuits, and dried fruit tasted good after the long climb. As they munched away, Neil tried to show Ryan and Kristi why over-powered CB rigs were a no-no.

He turned on the walkie-talkie to Channel 10. They could hear Road Toad talking to Italian Stallion, but they couldn't hear what Stallion said.

"See, he got through to Mr. Matucci," said Ryan.

Neil switched to Channel 9. A garbled version of Road Toad's voice came over the loudspeaker. Click.

There Road Toad was on Channel 8! Click. He was fainter on Channel 7, but his mushy signal still covered up all of the other voices.

Neil went from channel to channel — and there was Road Toad, his overpowered signal bleeding over most of the Citizens Band. "Understand now?" he asked.

"Oh, wow," said Kristi in dismay. "He's spoiling it for everybody else."

"Yuck!" said Ryan. "Can you imagine what it would sound like if all the zillions of CB sets were that powerful?"

"CB radio is for short-range use," Neil said. "An illegal amplifier gives one station an unfair advantage over thousands of others that have to share the Citizens Band in that area."

They finished their lunch and packed up. Then it was time for the trip down the mountain. It would be a lot quicker and a lot duller than the upward climb.

"Dad, can I carry the walkie-talkie?" asked Ryan. He tried to look innocent.

"He wants to listen to the skip," Kristi giggled. "He's a secret DX freak!"

"There's nothing wrong with listening," Ryan said with a frown.

Neil handed over the transceiver. "You can read the skip mail when we make our rest stops. Now let's rope up and move on down."

The Hawkins' began the journey down. It was the part of mountain climbing that all of them liked least. Going up was fun. Going down was just work.

So when they paused for rest, they all found themselves listening to the walkie-talkie. They heard CBers in Washington state talking on some of the channels. Now and then they picked up a Canadian from nearby British Columbia.

The most interesting eavesdropping of all came from the skip, and the skip was mighty choice that day!

". . . just because we're only 15 minutes from Disneyland, all Ruth's relatives from the East think they can use our house as a free motel."

"Breakity-break-break Skipland! You got the one Gila Monster-Boy from the Cactus Patch lookin'! Anybody got a copy on this Arizona star-trekker?"

"CQ DX, CQ DX, CQ DX. Santa Barbara 47 by."

". . . bring home a gallon of milk and some paper towels, and don't get stuck in the traffic on the Pasadena Freeway . . ."

"Yeah, come on Road Toad up in Washington State. You're sounding bodacious down here in Angel City."

"Break for a 10-73. We still got wall-to-wall bears eastbound outa San Berdoo, how 'bout it?"

The Hawkins family listened, spellbound. Ryan

switched from channel to channel on the low end of the band. Sometimes there was nothing but hash. At other times, the signals would be faint but clear.

Many of the signals were coming from places in California over 1,000 miles away!''

That was the magic of skip. Every CBer discovered it sooner or later. Usually, the radio brought in signals from not more than 20 miles away. If you were lucky, on a high place, or had a good antenna, you could drag in strong signals 50 to 100 miles away. Normally, that was the limit.

But when the skip was running, distant signals suddenly became stronger than nearby stations. Neil drew a diagram in the snow to show how it happened.

"The planet Earth has different layers of atmosphere. One of the high layers is called the ionosphere. It always has an electric charge. When the charge is very strong, the ionosphere can reflect radio waves, just like a mirror relects light."

The reflected waves bounced back to earth hundreds of miles from their point of origin. They could even bounce from more than one layer of the ionosphere and make a chain skip if the layers of air had a very strong electrical charge.

"But how come we seem to be getting more and more skip?" Ryan asked.

"Sunspots!" his father said.

Neil explained that sunspots were really huge storms on the sun. They gave off strong radiation. When the rays hit the ionosphere, they caused a powerful electrical charge.

"And the skip rolls in," said Ryan. "Ten-Four. I get it."

The weird thing about skip was, you never knew where it would strike! The skip-layer of the ionosphere could be 25 miles high. Or it could be 250 miles high. It all depended on the season, the time of day, the air temperature and the number of sunspots.

"The higher the reflecting layer, the longer the skip," said Neil. "CB waves usually skip at least 500 miles, but they can go much farther, too. The skip works in both directions, so stations at either end can talk to each other even if they're not supposed to!"

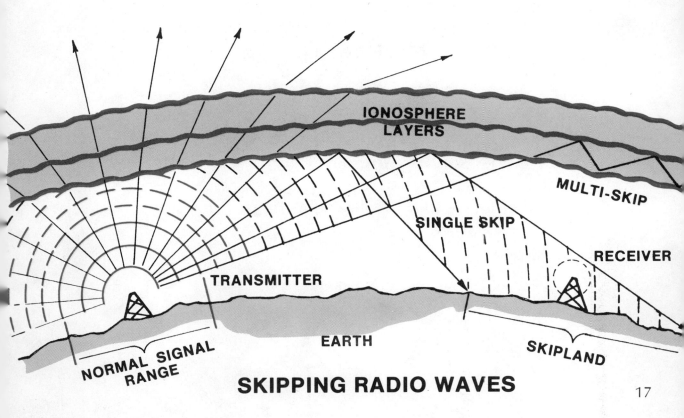

SKIPPING RADIO WAVES

"I don't see why skip-shooting is illegal," Ryan growled. "It's not like using an afterburner that smears other guys' transmissions. What harm is there in talking skip? Hams do it all the time. It would be fun to talk to people cross-country."

"The FCC thinks that skip-shooters will clutter up the CB channels," Neil said. "So the law says that you can't talk to CB stations that are more than 150 miles away from you."

"Some law," grumped Ryan. "If you don't use an illegal amplifier, who gets hurt?"

They sat there with the question hanging in the air. Channel Six gave out a buzz of distant stations. Then a clear, tempting little voice broke in:

CQ DX, CQ DX, CQ DX, Santa Barbara 47 is still 10-10 and by. What say out there in Skipland?"

Ryan sighed and turned off the walkie-talkie. His mother said: "Laws do change, Ryan. I can remember when it was against FCC rules to use CB radio for just plain chitchat. The Citizens Band was supposed to be for short, businesslike messages. But people wanted to use their radios for fun, too. So the law was changed."

The Hawkins family resumed their trek down the mountain. But Kristi had a parting shot for her brother. "You'll just have to wait a few years to gab with those beavers in Hawaii!"

That evening, they made camp in the back country of the Hoh River. They planned to finish the hike out on the following day.

Ryan sat fiddling with the walkie-talkie for a long time after supper. When the sun went down, so did the skip, and the mountain walls blocked out most local signals as well.

The next morning, Ryan woke before the others. He quietly crept from the tent. The pink light of dawn was just touching the high snowy ridges.

Ryan took the two-way and went to a high spur of rock. He climbed to the top, turned on the radio, and listened.

The skip rolled in! But this time, it was from the North. He heard Rusty Husky from Anchorage, Alaska and Eskimo Pie from Ketchikan. The best of all was a faint voice that turned out to be a climbing party on Alaska's Mount McKinley!

As the sun crept higher, the skip pattern changed. The mountaineers faded away. Half-asleep, Ryan switched to Channel 20.

". . . don't know how much longer we can hold out. For God's sake, if anybody can hear me, would. . ."

Ryan came wide awake. He turned up the volume as high as it would go.

The faint signal was smothered by bleed-over from another channel. Some skip-chaser was using an illegal amplifier.

Ryan fretted as he waited for the boot-legger to stop. He worked the deltatune of the walkie-talkie, trying to bring in the distant signal more clearly.

". . . locator beeper went out when she burned. I dragged Earl out, but he's in a mighty bad . . ."

Bleed. Bleed. Bleed.

Ryan shook the two-way helplessly. "Get off the air, you rotten turkey!"

After long minutes, the bleedover stopped.

". . . anybody can read me on this weakie-squeakie. Can anybody read this 36-Tango mayday? Anybody read 36-Tango, over?"

Ryan keyed the mike. "I hear you, 36-Tango! What's your 20? Where are you?"

The voice came back! The signal of 36-Tango was badly covered up, but the skip worked.

". . . from Juneau to Anchorage . . . fog and then the engine quit . . . in the snow . . . burned . . ."

"I can barely read you!" Ryan said, frantic. "You're riding into Washington state on the skip. Where are you, 36-Tango?"

". . . in the monument . . ." said the voice. Then the maddening bleedover wiped out the signal.

"Come back, say again, 36-Tango. Say again," Ryan cried.

Neil Hawkins voice was stern as he stood over his son. "Just what are you doing?"

"There's a mayday in Alaska, Dad. Nobody was reading him, so I worked the skip. I don't care if it's against the law. Somebody is hurt!"

Neil said: "Calm down, Ryan. If it's an emergency, you can talk to anybody. Let's try to raise him again."

But 36-Tango had faded away. The skip that had sent his signal to Washington was now sending it somewhere else.

"Did he give you his 20?" Neil asked Ryan.

"He said something about Juneau to Anchorage. Oh — and he said, 'in the monument.'"

"It's not much," Neil said. "But it will have to do. We'll 10-5 this information and hope for the best."

Neil switched to Channel 9. It was the official frequency for emergency calls. He tried again and again but he could not get any answer.

"Confounded bleedover!" he muttered. He went to Channel 10. There was Road Toad, happily fishing for skip with his overpowered transmitter.

Neil keyed the mike. "Break One-Oh for the Road Toad. We gotta 10-33. Come back to Sky Hawk, KCW-0484."

"Hey, guy! The Road Toad's gotcha. You doodahs fall off the mountain or somethin'?"

"We pulled in a mayday on the skip. A downed plane in Alaska. I want you to 10-5 it to the Smokeys, c'mon."

Sara and Kristi walked up and listened. Horror came to their faces as Road Toad said:

"Mercy sakes, good buddy, we can't modulate with any bears! We sorta running this bucket o' bolts in high gear without a glory card. Bears might sic the Friendly Candy Company on us!"

"Good grief," Neil said. "One of these guys is badly hurt. Just get on the double-L and tell the police this." Neil spelled out the pitifully few details that Ryan had been able to hear.

"Ten-Four on that, Road Toad? You gonna do it? Come back to Sky Hawk."

Silence.

"The guy threw the big switch," Ryan said softly. "Didn't want to get involved."

Neil said grimly, "Everybody pack up. We're going back up the mountain!"

Two hours after dawn, the Hawkins' rested on a high ridge. The Alaska skip was still running.

Neil tried again and again to raise an Alaska CBer. He knew it would not be easy with his low-powered, crude-antennaed two-way. In fact, Ryan's contact was almost a miracle.

But the miracle happened twice! A Juneau woman picked him up with her big beam antenna.

"He must be down in Glacier Bay National Monument," she said, after Neil explained the 10-33. "It's a wilderness. Right on a line between here and Anchorage. I'll 10-5 this right away."

"It's a load off my mind," said Neil.

"Call me later on the land-line and let me know what happens."

"10-4 Icicle Annie, KDYX-3622, down."

Neil sighed and turned off the two-way. "and now," he said, "it's time for us to go home . . ."

An all day hike to the road head. A late night phone call to Alaska from the ranger station.

Nothing.

Sleep. A long drive to the Hawkins home in Cascade City. Another phone call. Nothing. Sleep. Dreams of small airplanes crashing in icy fog.

A telephone rang in the wee hours.

Sara answered drowsily. The operator said: "I have a person-to-person call for Mr. Neil Hawkins from Juneau, Alaska."

Ryan and Kristi stumbled sleepily into the room as Sara handed the phone to Neil.

"Mr. Hawkins, my name is Barton," said a voice. "You don't know me, but me and my brother Earl have you to thank for —"

Neil looked at Sara and the kids. He smiled. "Found," he whispered.

"Both safe." Then to the man on the phone, he said:

"Hold on a minute, Mr. Barton. There's so much noise here, I can hardly hear you."

"Oh, that skip!" howled Ryan gleefully. "That was the most bodacious skip of all!"

CB GLOSSARY

AFTERBURNER — an illegal linear amplifier
ANGEL CITY — Los Angeles, California
BACKING ON OUT — stop transmitting
BEAM ANTENNA — a directional antenna with several elements
BEAR — police officer; also SMOKEY BEAR
BEAVER — pretty girl
BLEED, BLEEDOVER — interference where signal broadcast on splashover channel runs over onto other channels.
BLOW OUT WINDOWS — a powerful signal is said to do this
BODACIOUS — excellent
BOOGY — travel; go someplace
BOOTLEGGER — person operating radio illegally
BOOTS — illegal amplifier
BREAK — request for channel use
BREAKITY-BREAK — silly variation of BREAK
BUCKET OF BOLTS — CB radio
BY — standing by; waiting for contact
CACTUS PATCH — Phoenix, Arizona
CB — Citizens Band Radio
CLEAR — finished transmitting
COME BACK, COME ON — reply to my transmission
COPY — (1) message; (2) to hear or listen in
CQ — calling, an abbreviation from ham-radio telegraphy (a system of transmitting communications)
DELTA-TUNE — a fine-tune control found on better CB radios
DOODAH — impolite name
DOUBLE-L — short for LAND LINE; telephone
DOWN — finished transmitting
DRAG IN — receive radio transmission
DX — distant station, an abbreviation from ham-radio telegraphy (a system of transmitting communications)
EARS — CB radio
FCC — Federal Communications Commission, government agency that regulates and polices all radio operations
FOOTWARMER — illegal linear amplifier
FRIENDLY CANDY COMPANY — FCC; also CANDY MAN
GLORY CARD — CB radio license
GOOD BUDDY — common name for CB operator
GOOD NUMBERS — best wishes, from "73's," a ham-radio sign-off
HAM — amateur radio operator; person with more advanced radio license than CBer, able to use up to 1,000 watts of power, many different short-wave bands, make world wide contacts. Many CBers wish they were hams.
HAMBURGER HELPER — illegal amplifier
HANDLE — name used by CBer for station identification
HASH — static or other interference; also HASH AND TRASH
HIGH GEAR — illegal linear amplifier

HOLLER — call for person over CB radio; also shout
IONOSPHERE — a layer of earth's atmosphere that is electrically charged, located above the stratosphere
LAND LINE — telephone; also DOUBLE-L
LINEAR AMPLIFIER — illegal piece of equipment that boosts power of CB transmitter beyond 4 watts
MAYDAY — worldwide distress signal
MERCY SAKES, MERCY — exclamation of surprise, dismay, etc.
MODULATE — to talk over CB radio
MODULATOR — CB operator or CB radio
PICK IT UP — answer my transmission
PUSHING — transmitter power in watts
RAISE — make contact over radio
RASCAL — name for CB operator
READ THE MAIL — listen to other CB transmissions
ROGER-FOUR FER SHORE — yes; 10-4
SAY AGAIN — repeat message
73's — best wishes, a ham-radio sign-off; 88's — love and kisses
SHOUT — call for person on CB; also HOLLER
SIDEBANDER — CB operator using special transmitter; its messages can't be understood with common 23-channel CB radio
SKIP — bouncing radio signals off ionosphere, producing abnormal long-distance transmission and reception
SKIP-CHASER — operator who illegally contacts distant stations via CB radio; also SKIP-SHOOTER
SKIPLAND — distant stations coming in via skip
SKIP-SHOOTER — same as SKIP-CHASER
SMEAR — to interfere with transmissions of another station
SMOKEY, SMOKEY BEAR — police, expecially state police wearing broad-brimmed hats
STOMPED ON — signal interfered with; also walked on
SUNSPOT — storm or disturbance on the sun, producing radiation
10-4 — affirmative; yes; okay; message received
10-5 — relay message
10-9 — repeat message
10-10 — standing by
10-20 — location; also TWENTY
10-33 — emergency
10-73 — (1) officially, a smoke report; (2) in CB slang, a Smokey report
THROW BIG SWITCH — turn off CB radio
TRANSCEIVER — radio combining transmitter and receiver
TURKEY — silly or luckless person
TWENTY — location; 10-20
TWO-WAY — CB radio
WALKIE-TALKIE — portable CB transceiver or other radio
WALL-TO-WALL BEARS — police speed traps on highway
WEAKIE-SQUEAKIE — low-powered CB radio
WE UP, WE DOWN, WE CLEAR, WE GONE — one of many CB sign-offs
W-T — walkie-talkie

"LOOK FOR THE 10-20 OF OUR OTHER NEIL HAWKINS CB ADVENTURES"

10-7 FOR GOOD SAM

10-33 EMERGENCY

10-70 RANGE FIRE

10-200 COME ON SMOKEY

CRESTWOOD HOUSE

"KEEP READING."
IT'S A BIG 10-4 FOR YOU.